Fern Britton

A CORNISH CAROL

Fern began her career in television in 1980. In 1994, Fern became the presenter of Ready Steady Cook, which in turn led to her presenting the current ITV flagship show *This Morning*. Fern's warmth, humour, empathy and compassion have made her incredibly popular and she has become a much sought-after presenter and is now a *Sunday Times* bestselling novelist. Fern is deeply committed to a number of charities, in particular the Genesis Research Trust founded by Professor Robert Winston to help create healthy families.

She lives with her husband Phil Vickery, the well-respected chef, and her four children in Buckinghamshire.

By the same author:

Fern: My Story

New Beginnings
Hidden Treasures
The Holiday Home
A Seaside Affair

The Stolen Weekend (short story)

Fern Britton

A CORNISH CAROL

HARPER

HarperCollins*Publishers*
77–85 Fulham Palace Road,
Hammersmith, London W6 8JB

www.harpercollins.co.uk

Published by HarperCollins*Publishers* 2014

A catalogue record for this book
is available from the British Library

ISBN: 9780008103446

Set in Minion by FMG using Atomik ePublisher from Easypress

Printed and bound in Great Britain by
RR Donnelley, Glasgow

1

'Darling!' Helen dashed out of Gull's Cry and threw her arms around her daughter-in-law Terri as she headed up the path to the cottage door. Sean, Helen's son, was behind her, carrying their daughter, Summer, in her car seat.

Summer's chubby face split into the sunniest of smiles as she saw Helen. 'Gan Gan!' she cried joyfully and reached out her little hands for a cuddle.

'I can't believe how much you've grown!' Helen exclaimed. 'And is that a new tooth I can see?'

'Yes, and it's unbelievable the trouble that one tiny tooth has caused,' said Sean as they headed indoors.

He placed the car seat on the floor and started to undo the clasp that held Summer safely in place. The moment her granddaughter was free, Helen swept her up and showered her with kisses, which were returned enthusiastically.

This done, and after more hugs and kisses all round, they made their way into Helen's cosy sitting room, where Sean and Terri sank into the comfy armchairs with relief. The tell-tale signs of disturbed nights and fraught days were all too obvious to Helen as she took in the dark circles under their eyes.

'Teething can be a rotten old business for everyone,' she concurred, gently stroking Summer's flushed cheeks. 'Well, the good news is that Granny is here to take some of the strain. This Christmas, the only things you'll need to worry about are eating, drinking and making merry. We've got Piran on chef duty – he's a much better cook than me and he can't bear having me in the kitchen with him, which means I'll have more time to spend on you three.'

'You have no idea how good that sounds,' said Terri, gratefully. 'The cottage looks amazing by the way.'

'Thank you,' Helen preened.

Interior design was a passion of hers and she had lovingly devoted the last few days to making sure that her cottage really looked the part this year. The windows and doorway were wreathed in branches of fir adorned with twinkling lights, while giant candles flickered in storm lanterns on the window ledges. The banisters and mantelpiece were decorated with more fir branches and holly, and there were beautiful handcrafted wicker reindeer dotted around the room. Taking centre stage, the tree by the fireplace was utterly gorgeous; decorated sparingly with hand-painted sea-glass decorations that twinkled and cast dancing reflections of the crackling fire in the stove. The combination of fairy lights and candles gave the room a warm ambient glow, and the aroma of pine mingled with oranges and cloves, scented the air.

'It's absolutely heavenly,' sighed Terri, sinking deep into the armchair.

Tempting as it was to lean back and enjoy the chance to relax, Sean forced himself to his feet. 'I'll just grab the last of the bags and then I'll be ready for one of your legendary winter warmers, Mum.'

'I've added a dash of sloe gin to the mulled wine this year and I've got some mince pies warming in the oven – not home-made, I'm afraid, but they are from the new artisan bakery in Trevay and they're scrummy.'

'Amazing.' Sean gave his Mum a peck on the cheek and set off to get the rest of their luggage.

'You're all in the big bedroom!' she shouted after him.

'But that's your bedroom,' Terri protested.

'It's got more space and Piran and I will be quite happy in the little one, it'll be very cosy.'

'How is Piran?'

'Oh, you know.' Helen smiled ruefully, thinking about her grumpy, difficult, enigmatic, yet oh-so-magnetic boyfriend. They had chosen not to live together, both valuing their independence. He could be infuriating and unreadable but at the same time generous, exciting and sometimes completely magnificent. Lately, however ... Helen couldn't put her finger on it, but he'd been far more withdrawn and brooding than usual. Probably the full moon, she told herself. Nothing to worry about – yet ...

Helen checked her watch. It was gone five o'clock.

'Hope you both fancy a good laugh tonight. We've got tickets for the local am-dram panto - they're doing *Aladdin*.'

Sean struggled in with the luggage. 'Oh, great. All wobbly sets and fluffed lines as usual?'

Helen laughed. 'Guaranteed! I wouldn't miss it for the world!'

It was a packed house at the church hall. There were only three performances of the panto and tonight's would be the last. Helen's best friend, Penny, had landed the plum role of Aladdin. Penny was a hotshot TV producer and owner of Penny Leighton Productions, best known for her worldwide success with the *Mr Tibbs Mysteries* series and for her work on the Oscar-nominated film *Hat's Off, Trevay!*. Helen knew that Penny would rather be chewing her own arm off than getting sucked into yet more village bother, but she also knew that Penny took her role of vicar's wife very seriously indeed and that meant supporting the panto, all proceeds of which went to support the church's charitable work.

Also wanting to do his bit, Simon Canter, Penny's husband and the father of their daughter Jenna, had gamely taken on the role of Widow Twanky. Much as she adored him, Helen couldn't help but feel that Simon had been hopelessly miscast. He was a wonderful person – kind, decent and a thoroughly good egg – but there was no denying that he lacked the requisite bawdy humour essential for making the part sing. The topical jokes he'd been given about Kim Kardashian's bum and 'twerking' had fallen flat in the first act. And watching him now, holding two melons and doing a 'nudge nudge, wink, wink' over a 'lovely pair' was quite painful. It was hard to escape the thought that this was all rather inappropriate behaviour for a vicar. Penny was doing her best to carry the show, but she was far above her material, Helen thought.

Sean had opted to stay at home with Summer, who was a bit grizzly, so Helen had ended up sitting between Terri and Piran. A happy and animated Jenna was bouncing on her knee, shouting out loudly and eagerly every time her mummy and daddy came on stage.

Helen risked a glance at Piran from the corner of her eye. He'd barely said a word all evening, except to ask them what they wanted to drink during the interval, returning with plastic cups of orange squash. While everyone around them was laughing at the antics on stage, Piran's head was lowered and his piercing blue eyes stared disdainfully from hooded eyelids. His hand covered his mouth as if trying to stop angry words from escaping and he jiggled his leg impatiently. Clearly, his mood had not improved. Helen sighed and turned back to the performance.

Aladdin and Princess Lotus Blossom – who was being played by Lauren, one of the village girls – were making their escape on a magic carpet while murdering, or at least committing grievous bodily harm on 'Up Where We Belong', accompanied by the children of Pendruggan Juniors, who were pretending to be a flock of birds. What might have looked good on paper was somewhat let down by the execution. Firstly, the 'flying' carpet was supposed to appear suspended mid-air, not draped across one of the trestle tables normally reserved for serving biscuits and tea at church coffee mornings. Lauren was a well-fed lass and when she began giving it her all and belting out the lyrics, the table became decidedly unsteady. Secondly, the children shuffling onstage weren't quite progressing with military precision. Some were standing around looking bewildered, a couple of little boys were gurning at each other, and one little girl broke off and wandered to the front of the stage to tell her mummy she needed a wee-wee.

While the audience stifled their laughter, Aladdin and Princess Lotus Blossom continued gamely emoting about eagles crying on a mountain high, but their dirge was finally cut short when the shaky table leg gave way. Titters tuned to guffaws as Princess Lotus Blossom went arse over tit and ended up on her bottom, skirts in the air, with her frilly pink thong on show.

Tears of laughter streaming down her face, it was all Helen could do to hold on to Jenna, who was on her feet, screeching enthusiastically at the sight of her mummy rushing to help Lauren to recover whatever was left of her dignity. Rocking with mirth, Helen turned to say something to Piran, but the words died on her lips as she saw his stony face, eyes dark with displeasure.

'Well, that went off really well!' said Simon, happily supping at his post-panto pint of ale in the comfort of The Dolphin's cosy saloon bar and seemingly oblivious to the general consensus that this would go down as one of the most shambolic village pantos in living memory.

Penny turned to her husband, incredulous. 'Were you performing in the same play as the rest of us?'

Simon's good humour wasn't to be dented. 'I'd say it was at least as good as last year's *Jack and the Beanstalk*. Arguably, that was a lot worse. Don't you remember?'

'Oh, yes.' Penny shuddered at the memory of Queenie, who'd been playing Old Mother Hubbard, setting fire to the stage curtain while having a sneaky fag in the wings.

'Exactly! And we've raised over a thousand pounds from the box office, which will certainly go a long way to help with the funds for the trip to Canterbury Cathedral at Easter.'

'That's what I love about you, Simon – you're always able to see the positives in everything.' Penny gave her ruddy-cheeked, balding and bespectacled husband a loving kiss on his nose.

Helen couldn't help smiling at the display of affection. It was just the four of them in the pub; Terri had gone home to relieve Sean of babysitting duties, and little Jenna had fallen asleep, exhausted, and been carried home by Penny's brother, who'd come down with his family for the holidays.

'You're very quiet, Piran,' said Simon. 'How did you rate the performance this year?'

Piran kept his morose gaze firmly on his pint. 'No comment.'

'Not tempted to sign yourself up for next year?' Simon added playfully. 'Perhaps we could put on *Peter Pan* and you could play Captain Hook. You've got the perfect temperament for it and everyone loves a baddie!'

Piran glowered. 'Is that supposed to be a compliment?'

'No, no, I just meant—'

'I know what you meant!' Piran snapped. 'We haven't all got the urge to prance around like bloody fools for the merriment of others. Some of us have better things to do.'

Helen was shocked at the sharpness of his tone. 'Simon was only having a bit of fun, Piran.'

This earned her a fierce scowl, too, then, muttering darkly under his breath, Piran pushed his chair back and stalked off to the bar to buy another drink.

'Perhaps Prince Charming would be a better fit?' Helen said to his retreating back.

'I heard that *Beauty and the Beast* were casting.' Penny gave her friend a wry smile.

At this point, Audrey Tipton, the village busybody – a woman Helen always thought of as the love-child of Margaret Thatcher and Mussolini – came striding into the pub, with her husband Geoffrey, otherwise known as Mr Audrey Tipton, trotting along in her wake. Spotting Simon, Audrey held up a finger to her husband, as if commanding a dog to stay, then made a beeline for their table while Geoffrey hovered timidly by the pub entrance.

'Ah, Reverend Canter. I'm glad I found you.'

The sight of Audrey crossing The Dolphin's threshold had everyone's jaws dropping. She wouldn't normally be seen dead in anything quite so vulgar as a public house.

Simon got to his feet uncertainly. 'What can I do for you, Audrey? Would you and Geoff care for a drink?'

'No, thank you, Reverend,' she answered briskly. 'I'll make this as brief as possible. As you know, the Bridge Society Christmas luncheon was to have been held in the church hall tomorrow, but I've just been there and the hall is in a complete state of disarray. This really is quite unacceptable. If our annual luncheon suffers any disruption as a result, I shall hold you responsible.'

'Now, Audrey,' Simon's tone was conciliatory, 'you know that the panto has only just finished. I'm sure that Polly and all of the helpers are doing their best to get everything shipshape …'

'Well, their best clearly isn't good enough!'

'Give them a chance, Audrey!'

Over Audrey's shoulder, Helen caught sight of Piran returning from the bar. She was dismayed to see that the dangerous look in his eye had taken on new fire as Audrey Tipton delivered her rebuke. He and Audrey were old adversaries, their hostility mutual and frequently gladiatorial.

'Audrey.' Piran gave her a tight nod of the head.

'Ah, Piran Ambrose. Pendruggan's answer to Blackbeard!' Audrey turned to Simon again. 'Perhaps, Reverend, if you spent more time attending to church matters and less time frequenting drinking establishments with undesirables, this sort of problem wouldn't occur.'

'Now listen here—' Penny was on her feet, ready to defend her husband, but before she could say more, Piran placed his pint of Cornish Knocker on the table and rounded on Audrey.

Sensing what was coming, Helen put her head in her hands. Of all the times for Audrey to go rattling the bars of his cage …

'Now, Audrey, us undesirables don't care much for what other people think,' said Piran, his voice quiet but each word carefully enunciated and delivered with venom. 'What's more, we say what's on our minds. So here's what I've got to say to you, and you're gonna listen. I've had just about enough of your complaining, your constant interfering and moaning. No one gives a toss about you and your bridge lot – a bunch of stuck-up fusspots, thinking you're better than anyone else. Not one single person in this village likes you or wants to have anything to do with you. You're nothing but a dried-up old fruit – even your husband probably can't bear the sight of you, 'cept he's too scared to say so. So why don't you do us all a favour and take your bleddy whingeing and your bleddy whining and stick 'em right up that fat arse of yorn.'

The table sat in stunned silence as Piran's words hit home. For a moment, Audrey's mouth formed into a perfect O. She tried to speak but could only manage a strangled whimper, and Helen was horrified to see that there were tears in her eyes. As if hoping that they would leap to her defence, Audrey turned helplessly to the others at the table.

Simon was first on his feet. 'Audrey, it isn't true, we're all so grateful to you for all the things you do …'

But Audrey stepped away from his outstretched hand. With great difficulty she found her voice. 'Well. Good evening, Reverend. Thank you for your time.'

And with that, she walked slowly and with great dignity towards her husband. Geoffrey, who'd been too far away to hear the exchange, registered that something was wrong and hurried towards her with a concerned look on his face. Audrey merely shook her head in response to his questions and made for the door, head bowed. With one last questioning glance at their table, Geoffrey followed her out.

Aghast, the three friends turned as one to Piran.

'How could you?' Helen found it hard to believe that the man she loved could be so cruel.

'You went too far there,' agreed Penny. 'Poor Audrey. I know she can be a complete pain, but she isn't a bad person and she didn't deserve that.'

Piran turned to Simon, waiting for him to add some rebuke, but he remained silent. The two men looked at each other for a moment and then Piran picked up his woollen hat and coat and walked out of the pub without another word.

'I just don't know what's wrong with him lately,' said Helen, as much to herself as anyone else. This wasn't boding at all well for Christmas.

While Penny and Helen wondered aloud what could have caused Piran to snap that way, Simon sat in silence, staring at the door that had closed behind his friend, keeping his thoughts to himself.

2

Finally giving up on the doorbell, Helen stepped back for one last look at Piran's cottage before returning to the car. She climbed into the driver's seat, rummaged in her bag for her mobile and hit the speed-dial button for what seemed the hundredth time that morning. Piran wasn't at home and had clearly turned his phone off. Once more she heard the familiar robotic voice: *It has not been possible to connect your call …*

She pressed the Call End button and silently cursed Piran Ambrose. He'd volunteered weeks ago to come over on Christmas Eve and help her prepare for their big feast tomorrow. It was going to be roast turkey with all the trimmings, and Piran had been the one who'd insisted that the preparations would have to be done in advance if the big day was to be a success. Helen was making a simple starter of smoked salmon with prawn and salmon roe, but there was stuffing to make (Piran would never countenance anything so ordinary as Paxo, though Helen was a bit partial to it herself), parsnips and potatoes to parboil, giblets to be boiled and turned into stock for gravy – for which Piran had some secret recipe – pigs in blankets to prepare, not to mention their little ritual of injecting the Christmas pudding with another syringe full of brandy. They would be lucky if they didn't set the whole of Pendruggan ablaze when they lit the flame tomorrow, it was that potent.

It wasn't the end of the world that Piran hadn't shown up as arranged, but after last night's rotten business with Audrey at the pub, Helen couldn't help but feel anxious about him. She gazed up at his window and let out another sigh of frustration. Trust her to bag herself a mercurial so-and-so like Piran Ambrose! But no matter how she tried to pass it off as just Piran being moody as per usual, she couldn't help feeling that this time there was more to it.

She pushed the thought away, reminding herself that Sean, Terri and Summer were back at Gull's Cry waiting for her. She was determined to see to it that they had the best Christmas possible, regardless of Piran and his moods. He'd just have to pull himself together, and that was that.

No sooner had she put the key in the ignition than her phone rang. She felt a thrill of pleasure when the caller ID flashed and she saw it was her daughter Chloe.

'Chloe, darling! Where are you? I miss you so much!'

'Mummy, hello, I'm fine. Everything is OK here.'

'Remind me where here is? I keep forgetting!'

'Oh, Mum, stop teasing! You know full well I'm in Madagascar. We've been exploring some of the most remote parts of Masoala National Park – you wouldn't believe how amazing it is. Tomorrow, we'll be staying somewhere there's an Internet connection, so I'll send photos.'

'Make sure there are some pictures of you too and not just the monkeys! I want to see you're all right. You're still my little girl and it's so far away, I can't help worrying. I hope you've got nice people out there taking care of you.'

'Everyone is lovely, Mum, and like me, all they want to do is help protect the environment here. We're trying to support the locals' efforts to stop logging companies from destroying any more of the rainforest.'

'Oh, darling, I know it is what you want to do and I'm so proud, but I do wish you were here with us. Summer is growing so fast.'

'I know, I Skyped Sean and Terri the other night. They reckon she looks a bit like me.'

'She does a bit, but she's got Terri's eyes.'

'How is everything else? How are you and Piran getting on?'

'Oh, you know what Piran's like.'

'Impossible?'

'That's the word!'

They both laughed. It felt so good to hear Chloe's voice.

'When are you coming home, darling? Whenever I see Mack on the beach messing about with his surfboard, he always asks after you.'

'Soon, Mum. Tell him soon.'

'I will, sweetheart,' said Helen. She could hear someone in the background yelling to Chloe to end the call, the bus would be leaving any moment. 'Bye, Chloe – love you. And don't forget to call your father!'

'I won't! Love you too, Mum. I'll Skype tomorrow,' Chloe promised and rang off.

Oh, damn, thought Helen as she started the car. *I forgot breadsticks!*

It seemed the whole of Trevay were busily stocking up on last-minute items, as if the shops would be closed for weeks instead of a few days. Helen darted in and out, picking up a few more crackers, some chocolate decorations that Summer could dress the tree with, more Sellotape, more wrapping paper and a big slab of smoked bacon rashers, which would do for breakfast on Christmas morning and for dressing the turkey with. As she went about her errands she scanned the crowds for a familiar face, but there was still no sign of Piran.

Heading back into Pendruggan, she passed by The Dolphin. Don, the pub's owner, was busily rolling a barrel from the back of his pick-up truck towards the pub. When Helen tooted, he abandoned his barrel and waved for her to stop.

'What have you got there, Don?'

'Ah, this, this here is me special Pendruggan Christmas Ale. Comes from a secret brewery that only I knows about and I can only get me hands on one barrel a year. Folks come from far and wide to try this. We crack it open on Christmas morning and it's all gone by lunchtime.'

'Secret?' Don's wife, Dorrie, suddenly appeared in the pub doorway, wiping her hands on a tea towel. 'Nothing secret about it at all. He brews it in his shed and drinks most of it himself on the day!' They laughed good-naturedly at this and Helen laughed along with them.

'Well, I might be along to try it myself.'

'Make sure you bring that Piran Ambrose with you 'n' all. He's quite partial to a bit of this.'

'I'll try, Don – if I ever find him.'

'Find him? Well, he be down on his boat – I were out over Trevay Harbour way and I saw him. Set to be there all day from the look of 'im.'

'Oh. I see …' Piran used his boat the way a lot of men used their potting sheds. It served a purpose that went beyond fishing trips – he used it as a place to think. Or a place to be alone. Why had he gone out there today of all days, knowing that she was counting on his help?

'Thanks, Don. Save some of that ale for me!'

'Ah, no special treatment, I'm afraid, you'll just have to be early doors tomorrow!' he called after her as she gave another toot of the horn and drove off.

*

When she got home, Helen insisted that Sean and Terri leave Summer to her while they had some time to themselves. They needed little encouragement; within minutes they'd grabbed their coats and set off for a bracing walk along the cliffs.

'And stop by The Dolphin for a pub lunch,' she urged as she and Summer waved goodbye from the cottage door. 'There's no rush to get back. Summer and I can have an afternoon together, can't we, darling girl?'

'Gan Gan!' Summer gave her another sloppy kiss.

Helen was pleased when Summer went straight down in her travel cot. Her parenting skills – or grandparenting? – were coming back and as she gazed down at her granddaughter's angelic features, she kept her fingers crossed that Summer's teething pains wouldn't disturb her slumber.

Putting her feet up for five minutes, she called Penny and told her about Piran's disappearing act.

'Do you think he'll remember our plans for tonight?' Penny asked.

That evening, the village green was to be given over to a carol concert and the entire village would be there. A huge Christmas tree decked with hundreds of multicoloured lights had been erected on the green. When darkness fell and everyone gathered round it, the atmosphere would be magical; it was something everyone looked forward to each year. Afterwards, they were all going to head over to Trevay for a curry. It wouldn't be that late, so Sean, Terri and Summer were going to come along too. Piran adored Summer, but he hadn't been in to see her since she arrived. *Stop it*, Helen told herself, knowing that if she thought about it too much she'd get cross.

'He'll remember,' she assured Penny, 'if he knows what's good for him. I've been looking forward to it for ages, so he'd better not let me down tonight as well.'

*

The rest of the day passed without a peep from Piran. Helen had tried his phone once or twice, each time with the same result. She kept herself busy, and tried to stay jolly with Christmas music playing in the kitchen as she ticked off as many of the necessary preparations as she could. She'd got out the ice-cream maker and had enjoyed making a rich vanilla ice cream. Tomorrow, she was planning to take some of the Christmas pudding and churn it in with the ice cream with a drop or two of rum. She'd then freeze it again into a block and then later on, when their dinner had gone down a bit and they were watching telly, she would cut it into thick slabs, stick the slabs between two wafers and serve them up as a lovely decadent Christmassy take on a childhood favourite.

Despite her best efforts, there was no denying that Piran's absence had taken some of the enjoyment out of it. Helen couldn't stop herself running to the window every time she heard a vehicle, hoping to see his battered truck pulling up outside.

It was now early evening and almost time to set off for the carol singing. Terri and Sean had enjoyed their walk and then gone for a little nap upstairs while she and Summer watched *Finding Nemo* on TV. When her parents started to stir, Summer had insisted on joining them upstairs on their bed. Now Helen could hear them all getting ready, singing songs and enjoying being together. It made her smile to hear them.

This time when she ran to the window at the sound of a pickup on the lane, her heart leapt as she saw Piran climb out, leaving Jack, his faithful Jack Russell terrier, gazing out of the window.

Helen was at the door before he had even got halfway up the path. He looked tired and troubled, but at the same time she could see that streak of defiance in his eyes. His black corkscrew curls were wilder than ever after being blown about on the boat all day and Helen felt slightly annoyed at herself for finding him incredibly sexy when she ought by rights to be angry. She only hoped he had a change of clothes in the car, because he was still in his oilskins and he couldn't join them for carols and a curry dressed like that.

He remained stubbornly on the path and when Helen opened her mouth to speak, he silenced her with a raised hand.

'Before you say anything, I'm not coming tonight. I've been working on the boat all day and I'm tired.'

'But why were you working on it today of all days? You knew how much we had to do – and you haven't even come by to say hello to Summer yet.'

Far from offering an apology, he glowered at her. 'Why do I always have to fit in with you?'

'What do you mean?' said Helen, flummoxed.

'You know what I mean. These things that we "have to do" are things that you want to do – not me. I don't remember signing up for anything.'

Helen found herself at a loss. Where on earth had all this bad humour come from – they were meant to love each other, weren't they? 'But, Piran, it's Christmas …' was all she could come up with.

'Christmas? What do I care for Christmas?' Piran's voice was cold. 'From what I can see, Christmas is one more excuse for folks to spend obscene amounts of money on useless presents that no one wants, and send each other pointless cards that spout glib phrases like "goodwill to all men" – which no one ever means, let alone acts upon. Christmas means nothing to me and will never mean anything to me, so I don't care about dreary carols on the green, I don't care about a mediocre curry in Trevay, listening to Penny drone on endlessly about zed-list celebrities in London, I don't care about Midnight Mass. I don't care about Christmas, Helen, and I certainly don't care about—'

For a horrible moment, Helen thought he was going to say, 'I don't care about you.' But she never found out what he was going to say because they were interrupted by the sound of footsteps.

They both turned to see a troupe of little girls in brown and yellow uniforms marching down the lane and into the village. Wrapped up warmly in hats and gloves, they were ushered towards Helen's front door by the jaunty Emma Scott, Brown Owl. There weren't very many of them, but what the Pendruggan Brownies lacked in number they made up for in enthusiasm and they could often be seen around the village, trying to win their badges for map-reading skills or road safety.

'Good evening and Merry Christmas to you!' Brown Owl said cheerfully. Helen returned the smile as best she could, despite feeling bruised by Piran's outburst.

'We're doing a bit of carol singing to raise funds for the pony sanctuary before we head over to the green to join in with everyone else.'

Without waiting for a response, Brown Owl turned to the girls and gave the command: 'Right, after three. One. Two. Three …'

Half the girls immediately put their recorders to their lips while the others began to sing 'Good King Wenceslas'.

Helen couldn't decide if it was the discordant recorders that were the problem or the funereal quality to the singing, but either way the performance was lamentable. Still, it was all for a good cause, so she darted inside to fetch her purse. When she came back out, she was dismayed to find Piran standing in front of the group with his hands help up.

'Stop!' he shouted. 'Just stop!'

The music trailed off and the children and Brown Owl stood open-mouthed.

'What's the problem?' asked Emma.

'What's the problem?' barked Piran. 'I'll tell you what the problem is. Without a shadow of a doubt, that dirge that you and your Brownies have vomited out is a crime against nature. A dying nanny-goat would sound more melodious than this lot! What badge are they trying for this time – systematic torture?'

For a moment, there was a deathly silence. Then a small noise came from somewhere in the group and Helen, already horrified by Piran's outburst, was mortified to see that the little Brownie at the front had started to cry. One by one, the other Brownies followed suit.

Single-handed, Piran had turned the cheerful little pack of Brownies into a wailing mass of misery.

Helen's shock turned to outrage.

'Right, Piran Ambrose, this is the final straw! Over the last few weeks, you've managed to royally piss off every single one of your friends and upset practically the entire village. But this –' Here she pointed at the Brownies – 'this is a new low.'

Having said her piece she stepped out onto the path and began to shush and comfort the little girls, while their leader stood by, dazed into stunned silence.

'Come on inside, girls. I'll make you all a hot chocolate and you can sprinkle marshmallows into it – won't that be fun?'

The idea of this yummy confection was already starting to cheer some of the girls up as she shooed them into the house.

When the last Brownie had passed through the door, Helen turned to Piran, who was standing in his oilskins, watching in silence.

'We all know you can be a moody bugger, Piran, but I've always believed that you're a good person. It looks like I might have been wrong. Maybe the message of Christmas does get lost sometimes, but turning yourself into a latterday Ebenezer Scrooge is much, much worse. I never thought I'd say this, but unless you have a major personality transplant, you're not welcome here. Not on Christmas Day. Not ever!'

She was about to head inside when she turned back for one parting shot:

'Oh, and for the record, Penny never, ever drones on about zed-list celebrities in London.'

With that she firmly shut the door behind her.

Turning on his heel, Piran marched back to his pickup.

Christmas, he said to himself. *Bah, humbug!*

3

The lock on Carrack Cottage was inclined to be temperamental but Piran had no patience with it tonight as he rattled the key in the hole, wanting nothing more than to get inside and shut the rest of the world out.

A traditional fisherman's cottage of grey weathered Cornish stone, Carrack stood in glorious isolation at the end of a dead-end track on the outskirts of Pendruggan, not far from Shellsand Bay. There was nothing twee or touristy about the place; the only adornments on the outer walls were an old gas lamp, which had been converted to electricity, and a distressed and battered life buoy from HMS *Firebrand* that hung on a hook above the doorway. This was his inner sanctum, and he had no intention of sharing it full time with anybody. Nobody with two legs, at any rate.

Jack trotted ahead of him into the low-ceilinged room and went straight to the tatty old sofa, disturbing the two stray cats who had adopted Carrack Cottage as their home. Sprat the tabby and Bosun, who was as black as coal, jumped down from their usual spot on the cushions, leaving a trail of cat hairs behind them. Piran often suspected they didn't care who lived there as long as they got the best seats.

The cottage was filled with old furniture that had seen better days, but Piran saw no need to replace or refurbish anything. It suited him just the way it was. Evidence of his profession as an historian littered every surface. Ancient rolled-up maps of Cornwall were propped against the walls and the dusty bookshelves were crammed with tomes on everything from local history to works by Pliny. And then there was the paraphernalia relating to his other obsession: fishing. The TV stood on a lobster pot; the hallway and the pantry leading out into the small back yard were cluttered with lobster nets, fishing rods, tackle and fly lines; the cooler boxes he stored bait in were standing ready by the back door, alongside his waders.

Still in the blackest of moods, he took off his oilskins and hung them up, then began rummaging through the cupboards for a tin of pilchards to feed the cats. Something brushed by his heel and he turned to see Jack, soulful brown eyes following his every move. He reached into the cupboard for a second tin of pilchards. They'd have to do for Jack as well.

The smell of the pilchards made Piran's stomach rumble, so when he'd finished dishing out the gooey mixture of fish and tomato sauce, he went to his ancient fridge in search of sustenance. The tiny freezer compartment was permanently frozen up and he stared dispiritedly at the fridge's contents: half a packet of unsalted butter, half a lemon and a bit of slightly tired cheddar. The bread bin was empty. Piran cursed. Of course there wasn't anything to eat. He was supposed to be staying at Helen's place for the next few days, so there'd been no reason to stock up with supplies. The phrase 'biting off your nose to spite your face' popped into his head. Dismissing it, he set his lips into a thin line and went back to the cupboard for a third tin. If pilchards were good enough for the dog and cats, then they were good enough for him.

'Nothing wrong with pilchards, boy,' he said out loud. 'Would've fallen on them like a starving man when I was a lad.'

He took the plate of pilchards, to which he'd added the last of the cheese, into the small living room, and turned on the TV. Settling himself in front of it, he took a mouthful of pilchards and decided that things definitely weren't what they used to be. Rubbing at his eyes as tiredness crept in, he decided there was nothing for it but to make do with the cheese alone.

He flicked through the channels: *Morecambe and Wise Christmas Special* – *click*; *Eight Out of Ten Cats Does Countdown* – *click*; some idiot extolling the virtues of lawnmowers on the Shopping Channel. 'In December?' *Click*.

The next channel he clicked on was a film, so old it was in black and white. Piran thought he recognised the actor, though he couldn't think of his name, but the story was instantly identifiable: *A Christmas Carol*. What was it Helen had said about him being a latterday Scrooge? Piran knitted his brow but continued watching.

On the screen, Scrooge woke to find he had a visitor: the ghost of his former partner, Jacob Marley. Dragging heavy chains behind him, Marley was telling Scrooge *these are the chains I forged in life … you do not know the weight and length of strong chain you bear yourself … it was as full and as long as this seven Christmases ago and you have laboured on it since …*

Christmas Eve – it was inevitable they'd be broadcasting this old stalwart. Nothing coincidental about it, Piran told himself, watching Scrooge cringe and writhe as Marley's spirit clanked his chains and listed his torments:

I am doomed to wander without rest or peace … incessant torture and remorse …

Overwhelmed with a deep tiredness, Piran felt his eyelids begin to droop.

Hear me, my time is nearly gone … I come tonight to warn you that you have yet a chance of escaping my fate …

Despite the pull of sleep, the voice continued, drifting through his drowsy consciousness:

You will be visited by three spirits … without their help you cannot hope to shun the path I tread … hope to see me no more …

Piran woke with a start, disturbed by a loud knocking on his front door. Disoriented and with sleep still clinging to him, it took a moment to realise that the cottage was in total darkness. Scrooge and Marley were gone, the TV screen was blank. The lamps were out and the only light came from the waning moonlight that filtered in through the front windows.

Another rap on the front door. In the darkness, Piran picked his way over the plate that had held his pilchards, polished off long ago by the cats, and tried to find his way through the dark. Flicking the light switches on the walls elicited no response, either in the living room or in the kitchen, and Piran wondered if the fuses had blown.

He was almost at the front door when he tripped over one of the fishing rods that was leaning up against the wall. Falling forward, he banged his head painfully on the coat stand.

'Bollocks!'

As he untangled himself, someone banged on the front door again.

'All right, keep your bleddy 'air on, will you!' he muttered, fumbling with the lock and wrenching the door open.

Only to find that there was absolutely no one there.

What the hell was going on? No lights or power and now a phantom at the doorway? Piran wasn't sure where he had got the word phantom from but he suddenly felt unsettled. There were no such things as ghosts, so someone must have been knocking at his door – but where were they now?

He took a step out onto the path and peered into the gloom. He could see no one, and when he looked up the road towards the village he realised that was in darkness too. His position on the edge of Pendruggan meant that he could usually see the distant lights of shops and houses – but tonight there was nothing. It gave the night an eerie feel. Almost as if the village had vanished and he was the only one left …

'Things look different in the dark, don't they?'

'*Argh*!' Piran nearly jumped out of his skin when the voice came out of the pitch-black.

Then the voice again, and light from a torch illuminating a familiar face. 'It's only me.'

'Bleddy hell, Simon! Where the 'ell 'ave you come from?'

'Sorry, Piran. You're not normally so jumpy.' Piran wasn't sure what he had expected, but it was a relief to see Simon's cheery face. 'I was knocking for ages. I knew you must be in because I could hear Jack scrabbling at the door, so I nipped round to see if the back door was open. But it wasn't.'

Piran rubbed his hands across his eyes as if to rub away the last vestiges of sleep that still seemed to linger.

'What the hell is going on?'

'Power cut. The whole village is out.'

'Shit!'

'Indeed. Are you planning on inviting me in? It's freezing out here.'

Piran grunted his assent and the two of them, using Simon's torch as a guide, led the way inside.

'Gimme that torch and wait here.' Simon did as he was told and Piran headed off to the pantry. After much rummaging and rustling, he reappeared, carrying a handful of fat candles. Handing the torch back to Simon, Piran proceeded to stick them into candle holders. Before long, the room was lit by gentle candlelight.

'Save your batteries,' he said.

Simon switched off his torch and sat down. Piran checked the clock; almost eleven. He'd been asleep for hours.

'What are you doing abroad?' he asked.

'Well, I'm worried that some of the villagers won't be able to get to Midnight Mass because they don't all have cars and the roads are too dark. I've got my car and I'm going to have a recce and see if anyone needs a lift.'

'So what brings you here?'

'Ah, well ...' Simon blinked back at him, abashed. 'I was wondering if you're all right?'

'Why wouldn't I be all right?' Piran demanded.

Simon hesitated, trying to find the right words. 'Piran, I know that you hate talking about ... well, things ... emotions and the like. All the same, we have known each other for a long time and I can tell when something is up.'

Piran turned away, avoiding Simon's eyes. 'There's nothing up.'

Undaunted, Simon continued: 'The last few weeks, you've been really ... pent up, and it's obvious there's more to it than the usual trademark Mr Mean persona that you like to hide behind. I can see right through you, Piran. Is this something to do with Jenna?'

At the mention of her name, Piran leapt to his feet and rounded on Simon. 'Why don't you just mind your own business? Maybe the rest of Pendruggan like to spill their guts out in the confessional, but I can do without your cod philosophy, Vicar.'

Though his words stung, Simon persisted: 'Firstly, for the record, I'm a Church of England vicar not a Catholic priest, and we don't have a confession box in Pendruggan. Secondly, and more importantly, I'm your friend and I can tell you're bottling something up.'

Piran glared at Simon for a moment. Then he sighed and sat down.

'I don't know what it is. I can't seem to shake it off. Feel like I'm fed up with everything. Christmas only seems to have made it worse.'

'A problem shared?'

'I dunno, Simon. Don't feel I want to share right now. Perhaps this is the way that I'm destined to be from now on.'

'Rubbish! You weren't always like this.'

'Wasn't I?'

'Certainly not! You used to be quite carefree when you were younger. Remember that year when we did the Pendruggan Christmas swim?'

'We've done it more than once.'

'Yes, but no other year was like this one …'

4

1984

Piran's face broke into a smile as he saw Simon walking down the sloping slip road that lead towards Pendruggan's harbour. He'd been sitting, waiting, huddled up in his parka in the wintery sunshine, having called Simon last night to let him know that he was back in Pendruggan.

After a warm embrace and the customary ruffling of each other's hair, Simon stood back and took a good look at his friend. Piran's skin was the colour of golden caramel, his black curls were thicker and more unruly than he remembered and his piercing blues eyes were glimmering roguishly. A long summer spent island-hopping in Greece had served only to accentuate Piran's piratical appearance and the acquisition of a small hooped gold earring finished off the look perfectly. If Simon hadn't already known that Piran didn't give a toss about his looks, he might have suspected he'd done it on purpose, but there wasn't a vain bone in Piran's body.

'Where did the earring come from?'

Piran grinned sheepishly. 'Can't quite remember. A few too many ouzos one night in Mykonos. More trouble to take it out, I reckon.'

'How was Greece? Feels like you've been away for ever.'

'Only five months. But Greece in winter loses a bit of its shine. The tourists all bugger off and there's no bar work to speak of. I was ready to come home, anyhow. What about you, Canter? You're as milky white as you were at Easter. What have you been up to?'

'Come on. I'll tell you over a pint at The Dolphin.'

At the bar, Piran ordered them both two pints of Best and a couple of packets of Smiths crisps, while Simon lined up a few tracks on the jukebox. Piran was more of a Led Zeppelin or Pink Floyd man, but Simon couldn't resist a bit of pop and this was a vintage year. Which ones to choose? He settled on 'Two Tribes' by Frankie Goes to Hollywood, 'Wild Boys' by Duran Duran and 'Wake Me Up' by Wham! – but that was chiefly to annoy Piran.

At the bar, Piran was accosted by the young barman, Don.

'Oi, Ambrose, where you been lately? Not round these parts, judging by that suntan. My sister, Jenna, been wondering on that only the other day.'

Piran hoped that his tan covered the flush that he felt in his cheeks at the mention of Jenna's name.

'I've been travelling, Don. How is Jenna?'

'Well, you're not the only one been getting themselves about. Jenna finished her teacher training and now she's been offered a job in London, she 'as.'

Don's older sister was the same age as Piran and he'd been attracted to her ever since he could remember. They'd been more than friends at one time, but somehow, with his years away at Cambridge and her teacher training, they'd barely seen each other since leaving school. 'That's great news, Don. Give her my best.'

Don's eyes twinkled mischievously. 'She'll be here in a minute – she's been helping out, doing a few shifts – so you can tell 'er yourself.'

The thought that she might be along any minute gave Piran a thrill of excitement that he did his best to conceal as he was joined at the bar by Simon. A moment later, the high-energy bass of 'Two Tribes' and Holly Johnson's nasal Liverpudlian tones burst from the jukebox.

'Oi, keep it down. This ain't the Hammersmith Palais, yer know!'

Piran and Simon looked over their shoulders to see Queenie, the local postmistress and proprietor of the village shop, sitting at a corner table with a port and lemon in front of her. 'Welcome back, Piran! Come and have one of me pasties as an homecoming present – you can 'ave it on the 'ouse!'

'Thanks, Queenie, I'll be over in the morning.'

'Here, Don,' Piran handed over a one-pound note. 'Get Queenie another.'

'Anyway, Ambrose …' Don picked out a bottle of Cockburn's and poured a couple of fingers' worth into a glass '… reckon you've been keeping a low profile these last few years 'cos you're frightened of getting beaten again on the swim.'

'That what you reckon, is it, Don?'

The Christmas Day swim was an annual institution in the village, drawing people from miles around. Most came to spectate, but many took part. For the majority it was nothing more than the precursor to their first brandy of the day, and a bit of a laugh – no wetsuits were allowed and some of the more exhibitionist participants ventured forth in the nude, usually to cheers of encouragement from the rowdy crowd. There were, however, a hardcore of experienced swimmers who raced out to the buoy and back again, determined to claim the honour of pulling and downing the first pint of the celebrated, home-brewed Christmas Day Ale from the special Pendruggan tankard at The Dolphin. Both members of this elite, Piran and Don had a rivalry that went back years.

'Maybe I've been doing you a favour by not showing up,' laughed Piran. 'Not sure how happy you'd be to have a bit of decent competition.' He eyed Don's beer belly. 'Looks like you've been enjoying the beers and pies too much, mate.'

Don frowned. 'Oi, that's not fat! Hundred per cent Cornish muscle, that is!'

Simon and Piran spluttered and guffawed over their pints.

'You might laugh, Ambrose, but ain't many in Pendruggan faster than me in the water, you included.'

'That's fighting talk that is, Don.' Piran said this with a telltale twinkle in his eyes that revealed there was nothing he liked more than a challenge.

'You're out of the running, mate. Leave it to the younger ones like me,' Don jeered. He pointed to the barrel conspicuously placed at the bottom of the bar. It was covered in tinsel and lights and a handwritten note stuck to it proclaimed: Winner takes all!

'That barrel ain't got my name on it yet, Ambrose, but come Christmas morning it'll be me supping that lovely golden liquid.'

Piran picked up their pints. 'Thanks, Don – here, have something for yourself …' He placed another one-pound note on the counter. 'Reckon you'll need it to buy your own pints on Christmas Day.'

Don gave him a two-fingered salute but pocketed the pound all the same.

They took their seats and Simon began filling him in on all the local news, but Piran was impatient to hear what Simon himself had been up to.

'Well, actually, there is something I've been meaning to tell you.'

'What is it?'

'Well …' Simon played nervously with a beer mat.

'Come on, man, spit it out!'

'Remember I told you that I was going to stay on at Oxford and do a Masters?'

'In Theology? Yes, why? Have you changed your mind?'

'Yes. No. Well, not exactly …'

'Oh, for heaven's sake!' spluttered Piran, infuriated. 'Tell you what, why don't I finish it for you. You've decided to do your Masters and after that you're going to become a priest.'

Simon gawped at his friend in astonishment. 'How did you know?'

Piran laughed and put his arm around Simon's shoulder. 'I've always known, mate. Even if you didn't. All those drunken late-night chats about the nature of God and the universe? Most men our age would've been thinking about nookie, but not you.'

Simon's face betrayed uncertainty. 'Do you think I'm making the right decision? You don't mind?'

'Mind!' Piran gave Simon a giant bearhug. 'I can't think of a better man for the job. You'll make a great vicar! And if I ever find the right girl, I want you to marry us – you can also christen any unlucky offspring I might have. And when the music's over, I want you to turn out the lights and give me the last rites. Mind? I'm relying on you!'

As if on cue, the door to the pub opened and in walked Jenna. She didn't see the two men immediately and made straight for the bar. Piran watched her nervously and rubbed his hands on his 501s.

'Go on – say hello,' Simon urged.

Jenna was even lovelier than he remembered. She removed her red beret, purple velvet jacket and crocheted bag, then hung them all on a hook behind the bar. Her hair was the colour of wet sand and it took a moment before her clear blues eyes spotted him. When they did, she clapped her hands and a smile lit up her face.

'Piran!' She ran out from behind the bar and rushed over to their table. He stood and she threw her arms around him warmly. 'You're a sight for sore eyes, Piran Ambrose!'

Jenna barely worked her shift that night, much to her grumbling brother's annoyance. When Simon headed home a few pints later, Piran and Jenna were still ensconced at the bar, heads close together; talking and laughing and in no hurry to go home themselves.

Piran and Simon jumped up and down and rubbed their bare arms to try to keep themselves warm. It was Christmas morning and it seemed the whole of Trevay and Pendruggan had come along to the

31

Christmas Day swim on Shellsand Bay, though the hardy souls who were willing to brace the Atlantic waters were vastly outnumbered by spectators. The ban on wet suits had separated the wheat from the chaff; although the distance between the shore and the buoy wasn't far, the water was only a few degrees above freezing at this time of year and it could be gruelling.

Throngs of people lined the shore, a barbecue had been set up and someone was serving bacon sandwiches while flasks of firewater were passed round; the mood was jovial and good-humoured; a gang of teenagers wore Santa hats and were singing a raucous rendition of 'Rudolf the Red-Nosed Reindeer', but in their version it was another part of Rudolf's anatomy that was going down in history. Conditions were good; despite the cold, it was a clear morning with just a hint of the morning mist in the air.

Don, already stripped down to his Speedos, came over and slapped them both on the back.

'It's colder than a witch's tit out here!' He laughed. 'Ready for a good pasting, boys?'

Unlike Simon, who was waiting until the last minute to strip off, Piran was primed for action, his goggles sitting on his head in readiness.

'Don't be writing cheques your butt can't cash, boy.' He poked Don's stomach good-naturedly.

Jenna joined them and put an arm around each of their shoulders as they towered over her petite and slender frame.

'Ah, my two favourite Pendruggan boys!'

'Who are you putting your money on, Jenna?' Simon asked through chattering teeth.

'I couldn't possibly comment,' she replied enigmatically, refusing to be drawn, but she eyed Piran's tanned and taut six-pack admiringly. Simon saw a look pass between them and decided that things had definitely moved on since their night in The Dolphin.

At that moment, the sound of a loud bell rang out across the water. The adjudicator was the landlord of the pub, Peter. He was holding a large church bell, the same one he used to call time, and was exhorting the gathered participants to take their places.

The men and women who were taking part lined up and, when Peter fired the starting pistol, they all plunged into the sea. The coldness of the water took Piran's breath away. The last time he'd swum in the sea it had been in the warm waters of a crystal-clear Greek lagoon, but this was something else entirely. He forced himself to focus on keeping his limbs moving and progressed quickly through the water. He sensed that Don was a little way behind him – they were both strong swimmers but Piran's active summer seemed to be giving him the edge today and his pace quickened as the adrenalin coursed through his body, energising his muscles. He approached the buoy and risked a glance around. To his surprise and elation he was well out in front. Don seemed to have dropped back.

Having reached the buoy, Piran turned over in the water and kicked off for the return leg. He passed other swimmers on the way, all intent on reaching the buoy, but Don wasn't among them. Slightly ahead, between him and the shoreline, he could see a figure in the water. His immediate instinct was to adjust his course in order to avoid a head-on collision, but then he realised that the person in the water was Don. How had he managed to get this far ahead? Stung into action, Piran picked up speed in the hope of overtaking him. But as he passed, some sixth sense made him slow and turn his head. It was then he realised that Don was in trouble, desperately treading water, his face ashen.

Within moments, Piran was by Don's side. 'What's wrong, buddy?'

It was all Don could do to gasp out two words: 'Can't breathe.'

Piran looked towards the beach, trying to make out the lifeguard, but it was difficult to see from this distance. It was going to be down to him to get Don back to shore – and fast.

'Right, here's what we're going to do,' he commanded. 'Put your arms around my neck from the back and I'll swim us to shore, like they do in the movies.'

Too weak to argue, Don gripped Piran as best he could and they progressed slowly through the water, Don's rasping and ragged breath sounding in Piran's ear. Piran was beginning to tire when Simon came alongside to help. Before long they were nearing the shore, where the lifeguard paddled out in his canoe to meet them.

Don puffed hard on his inhaler. He was sitting on a camping chair, wrapped in towels and blankets, flanked by Jenna, Simon and Piran. The colour was back in his cheeks and his asthma attack was now well under control.

'Felt a bit wheezy this morning, but didn't wanna miss it.'

'You dafty. You could have drowned out there,' Jenna chided, but she was too relieved that her brother was going to be OK to be angry with him.

'Just glad I brought this with me. Don't have much call for it these days. Thought I'd grown out of the old asthma.' He took another puff. 'But it's thanks to Blackbeard here that it weren't worse. Good of you to help out, mate.' He looked gratefully towards Piran, as did Jenna, whose eyes shone with admiration and gratitude.

'Anyone would've done the same,' he replied, scoffing at the suggestion his actions had been in any way heroic.

'Not sure they would have if they was in the lead and looking forward to that Christmas Ale.'

'Who won in the end?'

'Not sure … come on, let's get down to The Dolphin and find out – we can't have them drinking all that ale without us now, can we?'

With that, the four friends headed off to the pub, singing 'Rudolph the Red-Knobbed Reindeer' …

'Jenna never did take that job in London,' said Piran, the long shadows cast by the candlelight flickering against the living-room walls.

'She went to work at Trevay Juniors, didn't she?' said Simon.

'She loved it there. Really got a kick out of seeing the kids thrive.'

'I remember how good she was with children. Always giving of her time. Didn't she volunteer at the hospital over the holidays?'

'That's right – and she usually managed to rope in a few others as well. She was nothing if not persuasive.'

'Tell me about it!' agreed Simon. 'On one of my first Christmas visits home after joining the seminary, she had me dressed up as Father Christmas, giving out donated presents to the kids in the children's ward at Trevay's old cottage hospital.'

Piran remembered it well. 'Didn't one young boy accuse you of being a fake because everyone knew Santa didn't have ginger hair and glasses?'

They both laughed at the memory.

'Then there was the other Christmas.' Piran's face clouded over again.

'The one where she …' Simon hesitated.

'Died. That's the word you're looking for, Simon. Yes, the Christmas where that bloody maniac … The hit and run … Police never got him.'

They both fell silent, thinking back to that terrible time. It was Simon who broke the silence.

'Bad things happen all year round, Piran. Good things, too. Christmas is just a reminder of how we should be three hundred and sixty-five days of the year. It isn't always possible and we're only human, but we can strive. What was it that Scrooge said, after his moment of epiphany?'

Piran's eyes narrowed – what was this obsession everyone had with Scrooge?

'*I will honour Christmas in my heart, and try to keep it all the year.*'

'You're too idealistic.' Piran shook his head dismissively. 'Folk only care for themselves.'

'I don't agree with you, my friend. Look around and you'll see. There is hope and love everywhere.' He stood. 'Anyway, I'd better get going. Some of the villagers will be anxious in this blackout and might need help. I suggest you might do the same yourself.'

Piran followed Simon out to the door.

'Goodwill to all men is usually found at the bottom of a glass of mulled wine and disappears along with the hangover.'

'You're so cynical these days.' Simon turned to face Piran. 'I remember something that Jenna said to me once: "A man who doesn't keep Christmas in his heart will never find it under a tree."'

He pulled on his gloves and hat. 'Goodnight, Piran, and a Merry Christmas to you.'

Then he was gone.

5

Piran didn't care what Simon said, he was too naive and trusting to know much about human nature. He wasn't worldly wise. But his words had pricked at Piran's conscience – the vicar was good at that – and anyway, he was wide awake now and might as well take a walk out and see what was happening.

Taking a torch from the ledge over the front door, he headed out towards the back yard. Opening the door to the shed, he shone his torch in, knowing that somewhere in the plies of boxes was a heavy-duty rechargeable lamp that would be more useful than the small Maglite one. Piran's shed was not a shed like most men's; it served as a workshop, with a long workbench down one wall and a dusty and cracked window overlooking the fields behind. It was packed with fishing paraphernalia, as well as several carpentry projects in various stages of development. His grandfather had been a shipwright and carpentry seemed to run in their blood. One of those projects was a doll's house that he had been making for Summer. Recently, he'd lost heart in the project and had struggled to finish it. He comforted himself with the thought that she was too young for it yet, anyway. Turning away from the abandoned project, he began rummaging through the boxes, which held everything from spanners to old copies of *Sporting Life*.

'Where is the damned thing?' he cursed as he pulled another dusty box down from the shelf.

Some of these boxes had been here for decades. *What was in this one?* He placed it on the work counter.

He shook it – nothing breakable – and then peeled away the yellowed and no-longer-sticky Sellotape that had been used to seal the box. His heart gave a jolt as he saw the contents. A hand-carved and painted Nativity set. One by one, he took out the figures: a shepherd, a donkey, one of the three kings, Mary and Joseph … Finally, rummaging around in the bottom, he found the manger containing Baby Jesus. Unlike the others, this remained unpainted and unfinished. Piran remembered making these. He had lovingly created every piece and now here they were – forgotten and useless. When was the last time he had made some-thing like this – made it for the joy of simply doing it and because he could?

He sighed and placed the figures back in the box.

Eventually, he found the missing lamp and headed out into the night.

Piran had always thought that the light was different in Cornwall and tonight it seemed especially so. This Christmas Eve, the night was clear and the stars lit up the sky like a luminous carpet. The crescent moon was low in the sky and the dew on the grass shim-mered like diamond dust on the fields.

He wasn't sure where he was going exactly but headed in the general direction of the village. There was something about the surrounding darkness that accentuated the sounds around him. Not far from the headland, he thought he could still hear the waves crashing on the shore. This part of Cornwall felt defined by the sea.

He imagined this was how Pendruggan would have been before the adoption of electricity, with seafarers totally dependent on the lighthouse to keep them clear of the treacherous coast. Cornish folk had held onto the old ways for longer than many, and he remembered that even when he was a boy, some of villagers still made do with gas and candlelight, and horses and carts continued to be a fixture of village life.

Gradually, he left the headland behind and the comforting sound of the sea, and a silence seemed to fall around him as he neared the collection of houses that made up the village. It was almost as if the land was holding its breath for something. Piran wasn't easily spooked but he felt unnerved – was he being watched?

He heard something crackle behind him, as if someone or something had trodden on a twig. An owl cried out in the distance and the hedgerows rustled.

Watched? Or followed? He shone his lamp into the fields.

'Who's there?' His voice sounded strange to his own ears as it echoed in the silence.

Nothing. He continued on his way, shining the torch again.

There it was again, another crackle to his right.

He swung round, thrusting his torch over the dry-stone wall that separated him from the field.

To his utter horror, an unearthly, grotesque face loomed out of the darkness at him. Its eyes were two black pool of darkness and its mouth was a red gash containing sharp yellow teeth.

'*Dear God!*' he cried out.

'Keep yer 'air on! It's only me!'

It took Piran a moment to realise that he recognised that voice and, when he did, he immediately felt like a complete fool. It was Queenie, of course, the octogenarian proprietor of the village shop. Her bright-red lipstick and NHS dentures had taken on a rather sinister aspect in the glaring light of his lamp. She peered out at him from underneath a bobble hat that resembled a tea cosy. There was no getting away from it, though – her eyes really did look like two black pools of darkness.

'What on earth are you doing out in the dark?' he asked her.

'Sorry, Piran, did I give you a fright?' She gave him one of her trademark cackles. 'I was trying to find Monty – she's gone missing. Ain't seen 'er, 'ave yer?'

'Who the hell is Monty?'

'She's a stray kitten that seems to 'ave adopted me. I called her Monty when I thought she was a boy, only she ain't. Vlad the Impaler would have been a better name. Always out on the hunt, she is, but she's as black as the night and now we got no lights I'm worried she'll get lost and not be able to find her way back.'

Piran glanced doubtfully at Queenie's birdlike legs.

'Queenie, cats can normally look after themselves, even kittens. Little old ladies wandering around in the dark don't always fare so well.'

'Oi, less of the old.'

'Come on – give me your arm. I'll walk you home.'

They headed back up to the village, Queenie all the while calling out to Monty. Piran could see in the lamplight that, despite being in darkness, the village was a hive of activity. Neighbours were darting into each other's houses, some of them carrying candles and torches, others laden with Thermos flasks filled with hot drinks.

Shortly, they were at the village store and Queenie opened the side door and let them in. It was rarely locked.

'Come in and have a snifter, why don't ya?'

'No, thanks, Queenie. I'd better be off.'

'Why, where you going? Don't be such a bloody misery guts.' She grabbed his arm and dragged him through to the back lounge, where Piran was surprised to see Colonel Stick and Simple Tony, plus a couple of old lags, Bert and Sid, that he recognised from the pub.

There seemed to be a party of sorts going on in the candlelight and Queenie was thrilled when she saw Monty sitting in Tony's lap. The kitten was licking her paws and seemed very pleased with herself.

Queenie's back parlour was jam-packed with comfy old furniture and on every wall and surface were photographs of Queenie and her late husband, Ted. Piran couldn't remember ever coming in the back before; there was a cosy clutter to the place that brought to mind a gypsy caravan filled with trinkets, keepsakes, crocheted cushions and huge glass ashtrays. A warm and lively orange fire burned in the grate.

'She got a rat!' Simple Tony dangled the rat for Queenie to see.

Despite the un-PC nickname, Tony was loved by the villagers, particularly Queenie. When his mother had died, the thought of the poor lad fending for himself had bothered Queenie so much that she'd arranged for him to take up residence in a shepherd's hut, where she could keep an eye on him.

'Fer Gawd's sake, get rid of it!' Queenie cried, shooing Tony outside, then proceeded to make Piran a drink.

She thrust a Babycham cocktail glass into his hand, which was filled with a purple liquid. Piran took a sip and had to fight down his gag reflex.

'Nothing like a cherry brandy and Coke to give you that Christmassy feeling!' she cackled. 'Cheer up, Piran! Anyone would think you'd found a quid and lost a fiver!'

The others all joined in the laughter and Piran felt his mood lift a little. Maybe it was the cherry brandy.

Colonel Stick stood and went over to look out of the window.

'People have been so kind. We've had everyone knocking at the door to make sure we're all right.'

'Yeah,' agreed Queenie, pouring herself a generous drink. 'Polly's going to bring us up to church just before midnight. It's good to know people care.'

Having made sure everyone else was comfortable, Queenie sat down. Minutes later, Tony joined them, having disposed of Monty's conquest and opened another can of Fanta for himself.

'When you're my age, you're quite used to this sort of thing, you know,' Queenie said. 'I remember once, when I was very young, growing up in London, we got caught in an air raid. This would have been Christmas 1940 – that winter saw some of the worse bombing in the Blitz. We came from the East End, but my mum and dad loved Christmas and they took us up to Oxford Street to see the window displays. It was exciting being there. Even though the city was on its knees, it never seemed to stop people going about their daily business. I don't think I'll ever forget the windows in Selfridges – I'd been looking forward to seeing them for ages, the store was famous for its window displays even in those days – but the place had been bombed a few months before and the windows were all bricked up. I started crying and my dad made it up to me by taking me into the big Woollies and buying me a liquorice stick and a toy rabbit. Then we had our tea at the Lyons Corner House. That jam scone was the loveliest thing I've ever eaten. No scone 'as been as good before or since.'

Queenie took another sip of her drink, enjoying the memory.

'It was getting dark when we came out and the Luftwaffe decided they'd start early that night. The sirens went off and we had to get down below as quickly as possible. Oxford Circus station was the closest and we had to hole up down there for what seemed like hours. The smell of all those bodies could be a bit much, but there was never any argy-bargy or trouble – we was all in the same boat, you see. We sat around, singing songs, and Mum had wrapped up a bit of fruit cake in a hankie and we lasted on that and a bottle of squash between us. It was one of the happiest memories I've got of them – we all sang "Knees Up, Mother Brown" and "Roll Out the Barrel" …'

At this remembrance, she broke into 'On Mother Kelly's Doorstep' and the others in the room all joined in. Even Piran and Tony, who didn't know the words, couldn't resist humming along.

Queenie continued: 'Not long after that I was evacuated to Pendruggan. My mum couldn't bear the thought of being separated from me but London was just too dangerous by then.' She paused and took another gulp of her drink. 'It wasn't long after I came 'ere that I got the news they'd been killed when an incendiary fell on the house.'

Tears shone in her eyes. 'Bloody Jerries. Our street in Bethnal Green might have been a slum, but we called it home. I don't remember much before Cornwall, but I'll always remember that day out in London.'

She took a hanky from the cuff of her seventies nylon shirt and dabbed at her eyes with it.

'Thank God for the people around here. Good farming folk I was with who loved me like their own. I never went home again. Grew up 'ere and married my Ted.'

Queenie gazed at the photograph of Ted on the mantel, still sporting a short back and sides despite clearly being of pensionable age. 'I've been a widow for over fifteen years now …'

The little group struck up another song, 'Run Rabbit Run', and Queenie joined in.

The Colonel explained to Piran that they had been listening to old LPs on Queenie's ancient Dansette, but the power cut had put paid to that. The Colonel was wearing his customary blazer and MCC tie and his walking stick rested next to him on the arm of his chair.

'Bert and Sid are widowers, Tony has no family to care for him, but together with myself and Queenie, we make up a little family and we look after each other.'

He pulled out his wallet and took a photo from it, which he proudly showed to Piran. It was of a very young but instantly recognisable Colonel and he was with his regiment. They were all in their dress uniform, handsome and vital, seemingly with no inkling of what lay ahead.

'Many of us ended up in a POW camp in Korea. I remember one particularly dreadful Christmas when typhus had taken hold; many of my men were sick and some were dying. The conditions were dreadful, the heat and the insanitary conditions were impossible to describe. But we endured and we made the best of what we had. We put on shows, poking fun at the officers and of our captors and we even did a panto. One of our men, Pinky, cobbled together a little newspaper full of funny made-up stories about what was happening at home. I still have no idea how he did it – it was nothing short of a miracle.'

The Colonel stared into the distance, and it seemed to Piran as if he was gazing directly into the past – seeing Pinky and all his old comrades in his mind's eye.

'Pinky never made it back to Blighty.' He put the photograph back in his wallet. 'It was the camaraderie, the kindness and the compassion that we showed to each other that kept us all going. Many of my dear comrades suffered the same fate as Pinky, but for those that did make it home, it isn't the atrocities and the degradations of war that we remember now, rather the comradeship and friendship of our fellow men.'

Piran realised he had finished his cherry brandy. Perhaps it was the alcohol that was pricking his eyes, making them feel a little teary, or perhaps it was because he felt humbled in the presence of this small group. Despite the privations and hardships they had endured, they pulled together. They made each other's lives better by the simple act of just being there for one another. They made it seem so easy.

'Right!' Queenie drained her glass and stood up. 'Now, you'll 'ave to excuse my manners but Polly will be here shortly and I'd better get me face on. Come on, fellas – look lively!'

Piran said his goodnights to everyone and they all wished him a cheery and heartfelt Merry Christmas.

'You see,' Queenie said as she escorted him to the back door, 'all we have in this life is each other. Living through the war showed me that we're all just people. Christmas might bring us all together, but goodwill to all men is more than a phrase that you trot out once a year.' She planted a whiskery kiss on his cheek. 'You gotta keep Christmas going all year round.'

6

After the warm and cosy fug of Queenie's living room, the blast of cold air was a shock to the system. Piran pulled his jacket closer around him. Where to now? He felt strangely rootless and the thought of going back to his cold and dark cottage and being on his own again wasn't something he wanted to contemplate.

For the first time in he couldn't remember how long, he was actually craving human company. He checked his watch by the lamplight. It was close to midnight. Without being able to explain why, he felt himself being pulled towards the spire of the church. In spite of the darkness of the night, there seemed to be a light emanating from it. As he approached, he could see that the church-yard and the path up to the large open doors were lined with dozens of little tealights and candles inside jam jars, vases and anything that could accommodate a candle without being blown out. As villagers entered the church grounds, they all added their own candles to the carpet of light – a frost was well in evidence by now and the lights lent the damp air an almost dreamlike quality.

The light from the church clock still appeared to be working and Piran thought it probably had its own power source. He could see from the dial that it was a few moments before midnight.

People were still arriving at the church, which was also full of candlelight, and he saw faces he knew and voices he recognised passing through the church door to take their seats. Even though he knew practically every single person in the church, he was anxious not to be seen, so he ducked behind one of the ancient oak trees that lined the path as the final stragglers, including Queenie and her entourage, took their seats.

The clock struck twelve. The sonorous tones of the old bell rang out across the village and the organist struck up the opening bars of the hymn 'Hark the Herald Angels Sing'. The voices of the congregation drifted out into the night and Piran found himself being pulled to the entrance, the carol acting like a siren call to his soul.

From the doorway, he saw the backs of the congregation. In the crowd, he was able to pick out Helen, Sean and Terri. Little Summer was asleep on her daddy's shoulder, her face a perfect heart shape, and Helen was gazing adoringly on her granddaughter while singing lustily, her face glowing in the candlelight. For a moment, she turned her head and looked to the back of the church, as if she was searching for someone. In his heart, Piran knew that it was he that she was hoping to see – he held his breath, hoping he wouldn't be spotted, but he was well hidden in the shadows and Helen turned away, quickly brushing away the traces of disappointment before her family noticed.

Piran felt a sudden burst of love in his heart for them all. Why wasn't he there with them? Why couldn't he simply walk right in now and take his seat next to her? What was stopping him?

With a sinking heart he realised that he knew the answer – he didn't belong. Love, family and contentment weren't for the likes of him. That was for other folks. All of that had gone wrong for him before and it would go wrong again – he was a fool if he thought things could ever be different.

Resigned, he turned for home. But as he made to leave the churchyard, something caught his eye. Standing in front of one of the graves was a man. He held a storm light aloft and appeared to be reading the words on the headstone.

The man turned and looked directly at Piran, then held up a hand to him as if in greeting. Who was it? Piran slowly walked towards him and, as he approached, the other man held his gaze, never wavering or blinking.

As he neared, Piran felt a shot of recognition – he knew this man, didn't he? There was something about him that was so familiar, if he could only put his finger on it. The man was old, perhaps in his seventies or eighties, but it was hard to tell. His face was strong, and though it was heavily lined and weathered, his piercing blue eyes watched Piran intently. The man's curly hair was grey, but it would once have been the same colour as the few wisps of deep black that lingered on his temples and eyebrows.

Though he gave no greeting, the man continued to regard Piran keenly, as if he was sizing him up. Then he turned his eyes away from Piran and back to the inscription carved into the stone. He lifted his arm slowly and deliberately and pointed to the name. Piran followed the man's gaze and drew a sharp intake of breath when he saw the name inscribed there:

Perran Ambrose.

Piran knew that this spelling was a variation on his own name. The words below said:

Born 1843. Died 1911.

There was nothing else, no wife interred with him and no dedication or words of committal.

The old man's voice when he spoke was surprisingly strong. The accent was unmistakeably Cornish and by its inflection, Piran thought he sounded like a local.

'You know the name?' He directed the question at Piran, but kept his eyes focused on the headstone.

'Of course I know the name.' How could he not?

'Then you know the name of Ambrose goes back generations here in Pendruggan.'

'Yes. It's an old Pendruggan name,' Piran answered warily, unsure where this was going.

'And you also know the meaning of the name Perran?'

Piran was about to reply testily that of course he knew that too, he was a historian for goodness' sake. But something stopped him.

'It means …' He hesitated. 'It means dark one.'

'That it does.' The man turned his face towards Piran. Now he was closer, Piran could see that the man's eyes, while a vibrant if watery blue, were somehow empty – blank – almost soulless.

The man continued: 'Many Ambrose men have been true to their natures. They like to entertain dark thoughts and shun the cosy comforts of life that other men embrace. There's many of the Cornish Ambrose men chose to live alone, refusing family and the company of their fellow men.'

Piran was filled with the urge to defend the Ambrose men, to say that that there were as many who made good lives and loved their wives and their children and were likewise loved in return, but the words refused to come out.

'Let me tell you about this Perran Ambrose that lies here,' the man went on. 'He was a fisherman who worked the waters in and around Pendruggan, lived out on his own in a cottage by the headland. He kept himself to himself; he bothered no one and no one bothered him. Came and sold his fish on the harbour, but pocketed his money and then went 'ome. He wasn't one for alehouses nor merrymaking.'

Piran longed to walk away and to hear no more of this story, but his feet were rooted to the spot. His gaze was locked on the man's eyes, which reflected the flickering lights from the candles.

'One Christmas Eve, there was a terrible shipwreck off the coast; the HMS *Firebrand* was caught in a terrible storm and driven onto the rocks. It was a dreadful night; dead bodies filled the water before being claimed by the waves, but there were many who clung to the wreckage. The villagers heard their cries and brought out their boats, risking their own lives to come to the aid of those in the water, picking them up and bringing them safely to shore, many seemingly more dead than alive. But not Perran Ambrose.'

Here he paused for a moment.

'What did he do?' Piran heard himself ask, though he was almost afraid of the answer.

'He refused to help. Kept his cottage door shut and his boat in harbour, despite desperate entreaties for him to come and help. His fishing boat could have taken many men had he come to their aid; no doubt many more lives would have been saved.'

They were both silent.

'How do you know all this?'

'You won't find everything you need to know inside the pages of a history book!' the man snapped.

How could he possibly know that Piran was an historian?

'After that, the name Ambrose came to mean something darker in Pendruggan. Perran Ambrose was shunned. No one wanted the fish he brought to harbour. Over time, folks stopped seeing him about. Eventually, they forgot he existed. Then one day he took his boat out and never came back. His body was washed up some time later and he was laid to rest here with no one to mourn him.'

Piran knew that the chill he felt was not merely from the cold air around him. The thought of this man, this Perran

Ambrose who shut himself away from life and from his fellow men – who had ceased to care to the extent that he would watch other men drown …

'But all that was a long time ago and folks forget.' The man turned once again to Piran and this time he saw something else in those eyes – sorrow? regret?

'They do well to remember and learn the lessons from the past.'

With this, the man turned his back on Piran and the grave of Perran Ambrose and set off down the path away from the church and towards the road.

'But who are you?' Piran shouted after him. 'What is your name?'

The man turned one last time and, as he did so, the lamp he held illuminated a small gold hooped earring in his ear.

Piran's heart froze as the man said, 'They call me Ambrose.'

He watched until the light disappeared into the frozen night air. When at last he turned his eyes up towards the clock, he saw that it was just after midnight. Like a radio being tuned in, the strains of 'Hark the Herald Angels Sing' once more reached his ears. It was almost as if time had stood still.

Piran shook his head, unable to comprehend what had happened. What could it all mean?

He took another long look at the grave of Perran Ambrose and thought he now understood. Piran knew exactly what he had to do.

It was early, not long after 7 a.m. when Piran let himself into Gull's Cry. The house was quiet and still in darkness, though Piran was pleased to see that the nightlight in the hallway was now working, which must mean that the power supply to the village had been restored.

He took off his shoes and his jacket, removed his warm fleece and made his way up the stairs, the ancient floorboards creaking underfoot as he softly opened the door to Helen's spare bedroom, where she lay, fast asleep. He gazed at her for a moment, drinking in her pretty features; she was still youthful and, here, in the half light of dawn, she could almost be a girl of eighteen. His heart swelled with love for her.

The bedroom door let out a creak as it swung closed and Helen stirred. Sitting up in bed it took her a moment to realise that he was standing there.

'Piran, what on earth?'

Before she could say more, he moved quickly to the bed and enveloped her in his arms, kissing her passionately.

He pulled away. 'Please, Helen, don't say anything. I know I've been a miserable old bugger these last weeks and I'm truly sorry. You've got every right never to want to see me again, but I love you, Helen – forgive me?'

She took one look at his open and sincere face and her heart melted. 'Always.'

Folding her arms around his solid frame, she returned his kiss wholeheartedly.

'You're freezing.'

'That's because it's cold out.'

'It's warm in here.'

'Maybe I should get in?'

'Maybe you should. I can think of a couple of ways that you can improve on that apology.'

They had a delicious twenty minutes before they heard the excited chatter of Summer from the other room, wondering if Santa had been to visit. They hurriedly made themselves decent before Terri knocked on the door and she and Summer came to say good morning and Merry Christmas.

Summer threw herself at Piran, who gave her a huge cuddle, enjoying the combined waft of milk and talc that came from her hair and was unique to small children.

'Come on, Summer, let's go downstairs and see what Santa has brought us all,' he said. Then he gave Helen a peck on the cheek, jumped out of bed, grabbed his dressing gown that Helen insisted he keep there and bounded down the stairs.

Helen had never seen Piran this excited before. He was like a small kid, eyes shining as he helped Summer to rip open the shiny wrapping paper to get at her presents. There was a wonderful haul and Summer cooed at the sight of the doll's house that he had brought with him.

Helen was touched at the trouble he had taken. 'I had no idea that you were making this, Piran.'

The doll's house was carved in reclaimed beech and Piran had hand-painted it in a soft pink gloss. It was decorated with a climbing wisteria that he had picked out in purple and green paint. He had stayed up all night in the lamplight to finish it.

'It's beautiful. Thank you, Piran.' Helen touched his hand and kissed his cheek.

'I'll make her some furniture too, when she's ready for it.'

After that, he made them all bacon sandwiches and Helen poured glasses of buck's fizz so they could drink a toast.

'Not for me, orange juice will be fine.'

'Are you sure?' Helen looked at him doubtfully. 'It is Christmas.'

'I know that, Helen, more than you realise. Now, drink up. We've got some calls to make.'

Within twenty minutes, they had pulled up outside Brown Owl's house, which was on one of the new-build developments just outside the village. Piran rummaged in the back seat of his pickup and pulled out a large cooler box.

'What's in there?'

'A peace offering.'

Moments later, he was standing in front of Brown Owl, apologising profusely for saying uncharitable things about the Brownies' abilities.'

'I've brought you something for the Christmas table.' And with this he opened the cooler box, reached inside and pulled out a giant live lobster, which wriggled angrily even though its pincers were secured with elastic bands.

Emma burst out laughing. 'Piran Ambrose! You're an enigma, wrapped in a mystery, wearing a fisherman's jumper – what am I to make of this! Don't think I've ever cooked a lobster before.'

Her children came running out and were full of oohs and ahhs.

'Can we keep him in the fish pond, Mam?' her young son asked.

'And,' added Piran, 'as a further penance, I'll come and take the Brownies through their knots badge.'

'They'll make mincemeat of you!'

All animosity forgotten and with the lobster possibly not even destined for the cooking pot, they climbed back in the car.

'Where to now?' Helen asked.

'Audrey,' Piran answered.

'Ah,' replied Helen. 'She might not be as forgiving as Emma.'

'I'm aware of that. But I've got an idea.'

Arriving at Audrey's house, Piran took a deep breath.

'I think I'll stay in the car for this one,' Helen said, and Piran gave her wink and squeezed her hand.

It took a moment for the door to be answered by Geoffrey, who was attended by two yappy cocker spaniels at his heels, both of which made for Piran's ankles as the door opened, only to be unceremoniously yanked back.

'Get down, boys!' said Geoffrey Tipton, hauling them away before eyeing Piran suspiciously.

'Can I have a word with Audrey, please, Geoff?' he asked meekly.

'I'm not she'll want to speak to you,' he sniffed. 'But I'll ask her.'

While Piran spent a nervous few minutes on the doorstep, he turned to look at Helen sitting in the front seat of the pickup with Jack on her knees. She gave him an encouraging smile, but his heart hammered in his chest as Audrey came to the door. Without her battledress of tweed coat, headscarf and sensible shoes, she seemed small and fragile in her dressing gown and slippers. Piran felt for the first time that here was someone who was just like everyone else, with the same hopes and fears, but who covered up her vulnerability with an armour of bossiness and bluster.

'Audrey, I—'

'Please make this quick. It is rather cold out here.' She made no move to invite him in.

'I came to tell you that I deeply regret the things I said the other night.'

Audrey regarded him coldly. 'There are things, Mr Ambrose, that once they are said, cannot be unsaid.'

'I appreciate that, Audrey, and I know that you'll find it hard to forgive me. But I want you to know that we all feel … I feel … that this village wouldn't work without you. You're the oil that keeps the wheels turning and if it wasn't for you, this would be one more Cornish village like many others instead of the special place that we all know Pendruggan is.'

Audrey didn't speak for a moment, but Piran thought, or prayed, that he saw a softening in her eyes.

'Actions speak louder than words, Mr Ambrose.'

'I agree, Audrey, and that's why I'm going to prove it to you. One day a week, I'm going to put myself at your disposal. Whether it's ferrying pensioners to the old folks' lunch or weeding the flower beds on the village green, I'll do whatever you want me to.'

Audrey considered his offer. 'One day a week, you say?'

'I'll make it two!' he added recklessly.

She put her head to one side and after a short pause appeared to make up her mind.

'Very well. But I shall hold you to this – as your word of honour?'

'I won't let you down, Audrey. I promise.'

'Good day to you,' she said, and made to close the door but then added, 'Mr Ambrose …'

'Yes, Audrey?'

'A Merry Christmas to you.' She gave him a small smile.

'And a very Merry Christmas to you and Geoff,' he said, returning her smile.

This time, Piran found that he meant every word.

'Why, Piran, they're beautiful!'

Simon examined the figurines from the wooden Nativity set that Piran had set down on the steps of the altar. As vicar, he'd been up for a while; Christmas Day was the busiest day of the year for him, but he had a quiet couple of hours before the midday service and then afterwards there would be mulled cider outside the church, drinks in the vicarage and lunch with family and some of the key church helpers.

'I made this years ago for the children in the hospital. Jenna's idea.'

Piran picked up the wooden Baby Jesus in the manger, which he had finished painting in the small hours. 'I thought you could put them under the tree for your Jenna, Simon.'

'Where did you find them?' asked Helen.

'In my shed. When Jenna was killed, nothing else mattered for a long time. And by the time it did, I'd forgotten about these. Until last night.'

He and Helen held each other's gaze for a moment. She squeezed his hand tightly.

'And now?'

'Now they need a new home. Will you take them in, Simon?'

'Nothing would give me greater pleasure.' Simon thought of his own daughter, also called Jenna, and of how her face would light up at the sight of these beautiful figures. 'They'll have pride of place here at the front, where everyone can see them.' He turned his eyes from the manger to his friend. 'And, Piran …'

'Yes?'

'Welcome back!'

They exchanged warm smiles.

'Thanks,' said Piran. 'It feels good.'

'Where are you both off to now?'

'Ah!' said Piran mysteriously. 'We are going – and this includes you, Reverend Canter – for a swim. Grab your trunks!'

As they left the church, Piran asked Helen to wait for a moment.

'There's one more thing I've got to do. You don't need to come with me.' She gave him a puzzled look, but let him go.

Piran walked towards the churchyard. It seemed different in the weak winter sunshine and he was worried that he wouldn't find what he was looking for. But there it was, in the same place as last night – the final resting place of Perran Ambrose.

Piran knelt before the grave and read the inscription again. He rubbed his eyes and shook his head, unable to believe that what he was seeing was true. But no matter how many times he blinked and read it again, the words were there, literally carved in stone:

Perran Ambrose.
Born 1843. Died 1893 aged fifty.

Below was an inscription:

In loving remembrance of Perran Ambrose who on the
twenty-fourth day of December 1893 attended the shipwreck

of the HMS Firebrand,
which foundered off the coast of Pendruggan.
Perran Ambrose and other Pendruggan men selflessly set
out in their fishing boats to rescue as many as they could
and toiled for hours in order that they might save those
who lay in the water.
A mighty storm raged and while other boats were beaten
back, Perran Ambrose continued his quest, though he was
thrown from his boat and drowned, but not before many
men were saved who owe their lives to his sacrifice.

This headstone was donated by the men and woman of
Pendruggan
and is dedicated to his memory.

In paradisum deducant te angeli

How could this have changed in one night? Perhaps he had misread the headstone in the darkness, but Piran thought not. Other things had been at work last night and Piran was grateful for the change in his heart and for the new ending for Perran Ambrose. Perhaps it was best if he didn't question events too deeply.

As he turned to leave he spotted a small snowdrop growing in the grass beneath the headstone. It seemed to him a symbol of hope and of new beginnings.

'Rest in peace, Ambrose,' he said gently and made his way back to the car.

'You can't be serious – that water is freezing.' Helen and Penny watched horrified as Piran and Simon stripped down to their trunks on Shellsand Bay.

Sean, Terri and Summer, along with little Jenna and Simon's family, all marvelled at the throng of people lined up along the shore, eager to see who would win this year's Christmas Day swim.

'Helen, you haven't lived until you've swum out to the buoy on Christmas morning,' Piran said, laughing, jumping up and down to keep warm.

'I'll take your word for it!' she replied, snuggling deeper into her warm fleece-lined coat. She couldn't help thinking that he looked pretty darned good for a man of his age, six-pack still in evidence.

'Piran Ambrose, as I live and breathe!' Don's voice boomed out and he gave his old adversary a slap on the back. Don was now landlord of The Dolphin and was as much a fixture of Pendruggan life as he had always been.

'Don! Not taking part yourself this year, I see?' Don was well wrapped up in winter outdoor gear and Piran could see that he and his wife, Dorrie, were manning the barbecues.

'The days of freezing me bollocks off are well behind me. Think the doctor would have a fit if I even so much as contemplated it – dodgy ticker and all that.' He tapped his chest with a finger.

'Rubbish, Don. You're scared of the competition – like always.'

After a bit more joshing and banter, there was no time for further chat as Peter, still officiating after all these years though long since retired, rang his bell for the off.

Piran and Simon lined up with the rest of the competitors.

'Remind me why we're doing this, again?' questioned Simon through chattering teeth.

Piran gave him a dazzling smile. 'Because it's Christmas, of course!'

To the sound of deafening cheers, Piran raised his pint of Christmas Ale to his lips and took a long, satisfying draw.

'Now that, is pure Ambrosia – excuse the pun!' Piran thought that nothing had ever tasted so good before.

Helen threw her arms around him for the hundredth time.

'I can't believe you won!'

'Neither can I!'

'It was incredible, you were miles ahead of everyone else. How on earth did you do it?'

'I've no idea – perhaps this year I'm just blessed. I feel blessed, anyway.' He gave her a loving kiss on the head and then raised his voice to be heard above the crowd of voices in The Dolphin.

'To make up for being such a grumpy old wanker, I promise that if Audrey will let me, I'll give Pendruggan their best ever Window Twanky in next year's panto!' This news was greeted by whoops and cheers from the whole pub.

'And I'd like to dedicate my win and this wonderful pint of Pendruggan Christmas Ale to all of the Piran Ambroses past, present and future who never forgot and never will forget what goodwill to all men really means.'

He downed his drink. 'Merry Christmas!'

Make sure you look out for
Fern's brilliant new novel,

A Good
Catch

Coming in spring 2015 . . .